# JACOB

LITTLE CAT TALES

BY SVEN HARTMANN
AND THOMAS HÄRTNER

EDITED BY JACK BERNARD

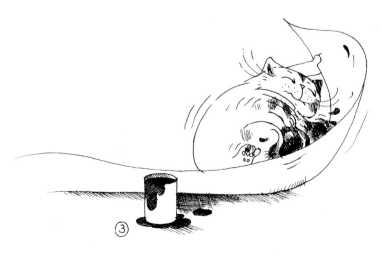

## LITTLE CAT TALES

BY SVEN HARTMANN
AND THOMAS HÄRTNER

EDITED BY JACK BERNARD
TRANSLATED BY ANGELIKA MACRI

BARRON'S   Woodbury, New York

© 1974, 1977 BENTELI VERLAG, 3011 Berne, Switzerland
PRINTED IN HONG KONG

### THE HARD PART: GETTING STARTED

WHEN you live with somebody, you have to learn how to cope. That's why I pay so much attention to my Human.

Humans need a lot of help. I had to help mine from the very beginning. And I guess that's a good place to start: at the beginning.

THE beginning was a long time ago, and I must have been very young. I can hardly remember it. My mother was there, I know, and my brothers and sisters, and everything was nice and warm, and we had a lot to eat.

THEN, one day, a Human came. She had big funny eyes and big funny claws that were all red and stayed out all the time. And she smelled funny. This Human took me and put me in a dark box with holes in it. The holes weren't big enough for me to crawl through, and I was really scared. I cried a lot, but it didn't do any good. I was warm in the box, but I was all alone, and the box kept swaying from side to side. I was still afraid, but I stopped crying because I wanted the Human to think I was brave.

SUDDENLY, the box stopped swaying, and I heard voices. Then the box opened. I saw the Human with the red claws and, next to her, another Human. This one had hair all over where Humans have their faces. His teeth showed from behind the hair, and he made sounds — laughing, they call it. (I found that out later.) Then the red-claw Human laughed too, and they rubbed their heads together and made smacking noises.

THE new Human — I guess I can call him *my* Human now — lifted me out of the box. I tried to hold on to it, but he took me out anyway.

THEN he began rubbing my head and neck with the tips of his claws. It felt good.
Almost as good as when my mother used to wash me, except that she used her tongue.
I soon found out that when Humans do that, they don't call it washing. They call it petting.
Anyhow, it felt good, and I wasn't scared any more. As soon as my Human put
me down, I decided to look around.

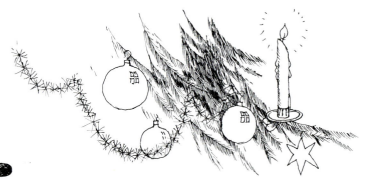

THE first thing I saw was a big green — a tree, they call it. This tree had really sharp
leaves, like needles, that hurt my nose when I tried to smell them. And it
had round shiny balls all over it, and yellow sticks with lights at
the top that felt hot and burned. I decided that I'd better leave the tree alone.

PRETTY soon, the Humans gave me a saucer of milk, but I didn't
want it. I was too excited to eat. I wanted to play with the blue ribbon on my
box. I fought hard, and the ribbon kept trying to tie me up again. But I won. The Human
with the hair laughed so loud that he scared me all over again. But I was so tired that I almost fell
asleep right in the middle of being scared.

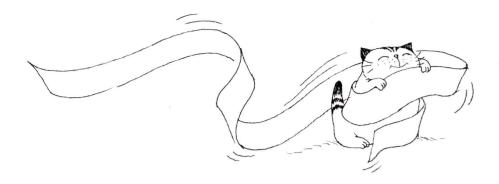

THEN the Human picked me up and put me inside his shirt where it was all furry and warm. He rubbed me with his claws again and made nice, soft sounds, and I wasn't afraid any more.

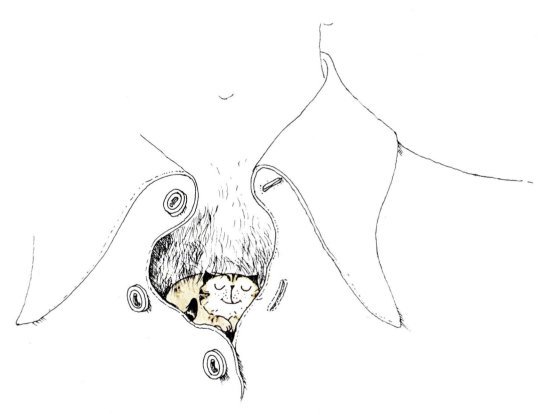

IT was then I decided he was really going to be MY Human and nobody else's. I think he likes belonging to me, because he's never tried to run away.

## MY HUMAN AND ME

WHEN I came to live here, I was still very small, but I already had whiskers. Whiskers are something you have on your face to keep you from bumping into things. They are really nice, and I'm as proud as I can be of mine.

IN those days, my tail was pretty small too, and it stood straight up. I kept trying to catch it, but I couldn't. My Human used to laugh at that a lot, so I gave up. I still do it sometimes, but only when he isn't looking. I don't know why he thinks my tail is funny. What's really funny is his whole body. And especially his feet. He can *change* them. Sometimes they're white and soft, and sometimes they're hard and black and shiny.

HE's very high, too. But I like that, because I get to climb on him. When I do, he lets out these strange, shrill sounds — like me when I used to cry, but a lot louder. The sounds are funny, and I laugh when he makes them.

MY Human has his eyes at the top of his body. They're funny too, but not the kind of funny makes me laugh. *Strange* funny. I don't like to look at them. When he looks at me, I try not to see his eyes. I look at his ears instead. I wonder if he notices.

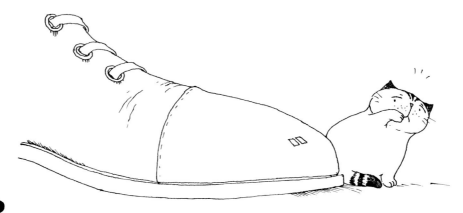

FRANKLY, the ears aren't much better. They're not pointed, and they're all full of wrinkles. Worst of all, he can't even move them. What good are they?

But that's not all. Sometimes my Human smells bad. That happens especially when he puts a little white stick in his mouth and the stick burns up. Then some kind of white fog comes out of his mouth. It has a strong, bad smell, and it hurts my eyes. Sometimes it tickles my nose too, and I have to sneeze. Then he laughs at me.

My Human can make nice, soft sounds, and when he does, I show him I like the sounds by rubbing against his legs or lying down on his feet. But sometimes the sounds get loud and are not nice at all, and I jump up and run away from him. Then they get soft again — this just shows that Humans are capable of learning if you're strict enough with them.

The nicest part of my Human are his paws. He has claws, but they're not hard and sharp like mine. They're soft and long, and they bend.
My Human uses his claws to scratch me and rub me all over. Sometimes he rubs me where I can't reach to wash myself so well. But he also does it on my tail, and my stomach, and all over my back. That feels good, and when he does it, I like to sing to myself. Sometimes I fall asleep.

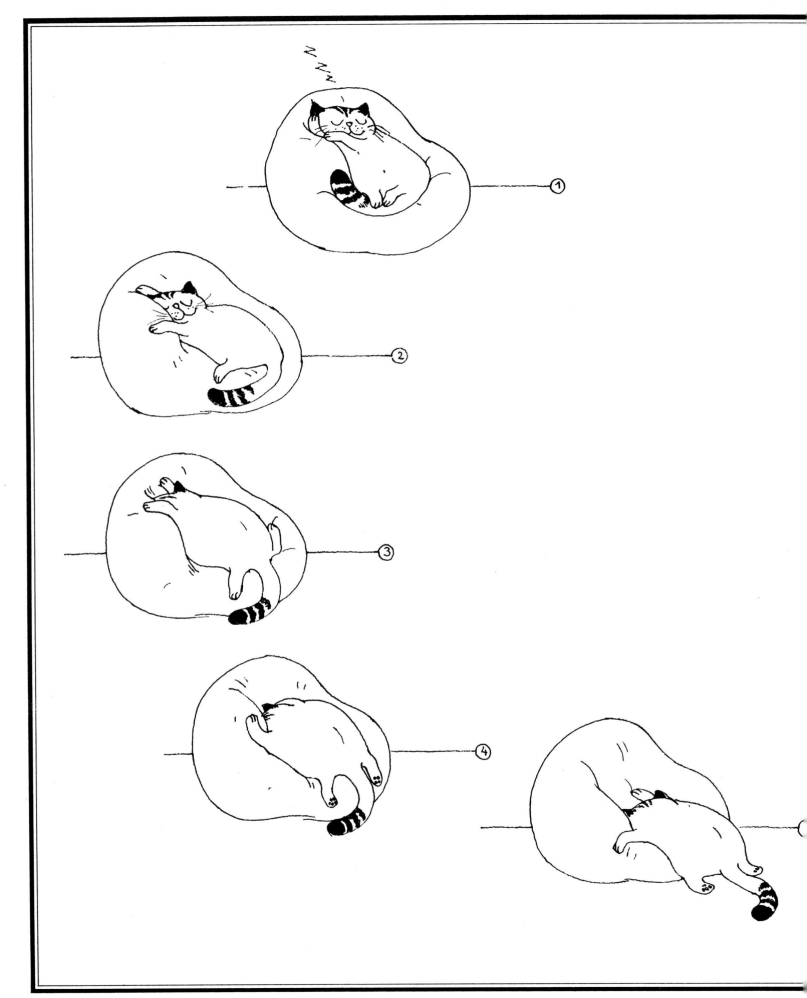

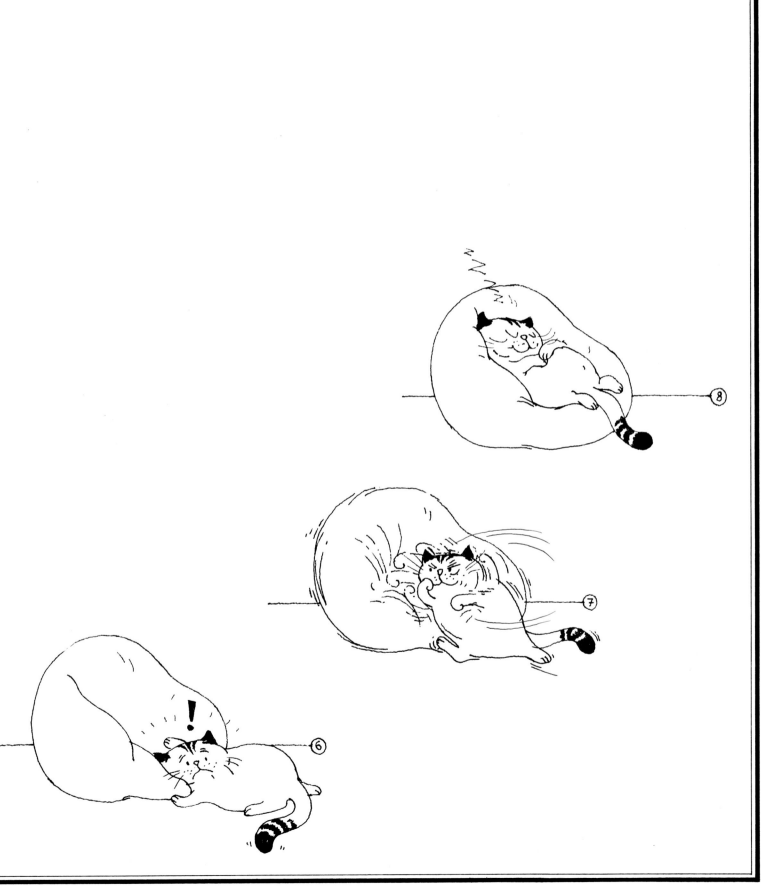

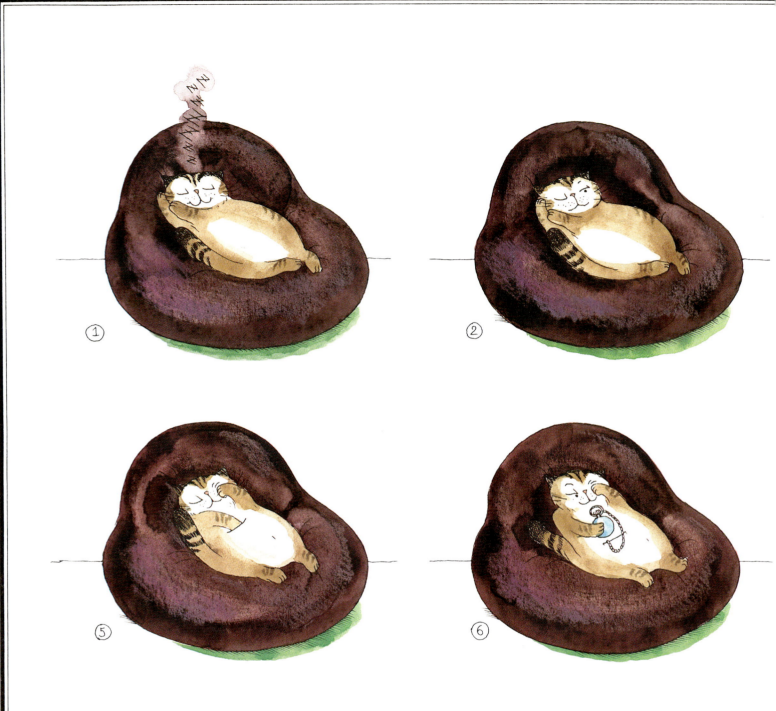

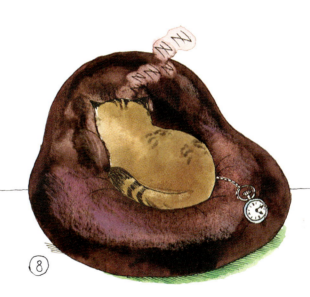

# MY HUMAN RATTLES HIS CAGE

When I was little, my Human called me "Purr." This is the word they use for the sounds I make when I'm singing. Don't ask me why. He'd pet me, and I'd "purr." So, he called me Purr. I liked being called Purr.

The thing about a Human is that you can never tell which way he'll jump. Sometimes it was Purr-this and Purr-that, and everything was soft and nice. Then, for no reason, the screaming and yelling would start. Usually, it happened when I did something that showed I was better than he was at something. For instance, I never bump into things in the dark. But he's *always* bumping into things, and then the yelling starts.

I did everything I could to keep my Human from finding out that I am smarter than he is. But it was too obvious, and he just couldn't stand it. Then he would really yell a lot, even for the least little thing. Like this coat he wears every morning. I like to pull out the threads on it, because it looks so much better with all those threads hanging down. You'd have thought I was trying to burn the house down, the way he carried on. That proves not only that he's not very smart, but that he doesn't have much taste, either.

Maybe you're wondering what all this has to do with the name "Purr." It's like this: when my Human yelled at me, he kept calling me Purr. Purr is a very hard word to yell, even if you try. And it's a nice, soft word, even when you don't want it to be nice and soft. So, one day, I suddenly found that my name had been changed to "Jacob." At first, I made believe that I didn't know who he was talking to, but that didn't work. So I had to get used to being called Jacob.

If there's one thing my Human is good at, it's saying "Jacob" in a lot of different ways. Sometimes he says it "Jaaaaaacooob," all stretched out. And then I know something bad is coming, even when he says it softly. Sometimes he says it real short and angry: "JA-cob!" That's when I run and hide. Other times, it's "Jaaa-cob," with the "-cob" real short; then I know he thinks I'm up to something that he doesn't like. (*How he knows, I've never been able to figure out.*)

Sometimes I'm glad when my Human goes out and leaves me alone for a while. Then I can get things done without always getting yelled at. When he gets home, he calls me and calls me, saying "Jacob" in all kinds of ways. But I pretend I don't know he's home yet. There's no point in letting him know how smart I really am. He'd only be jealous.

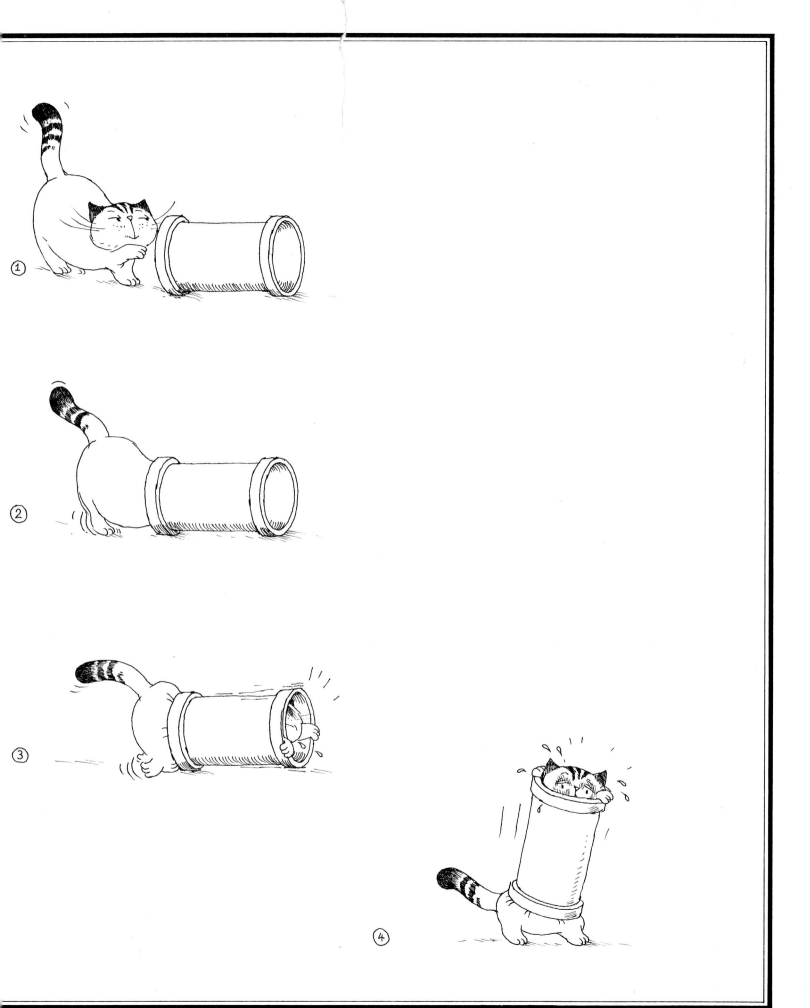

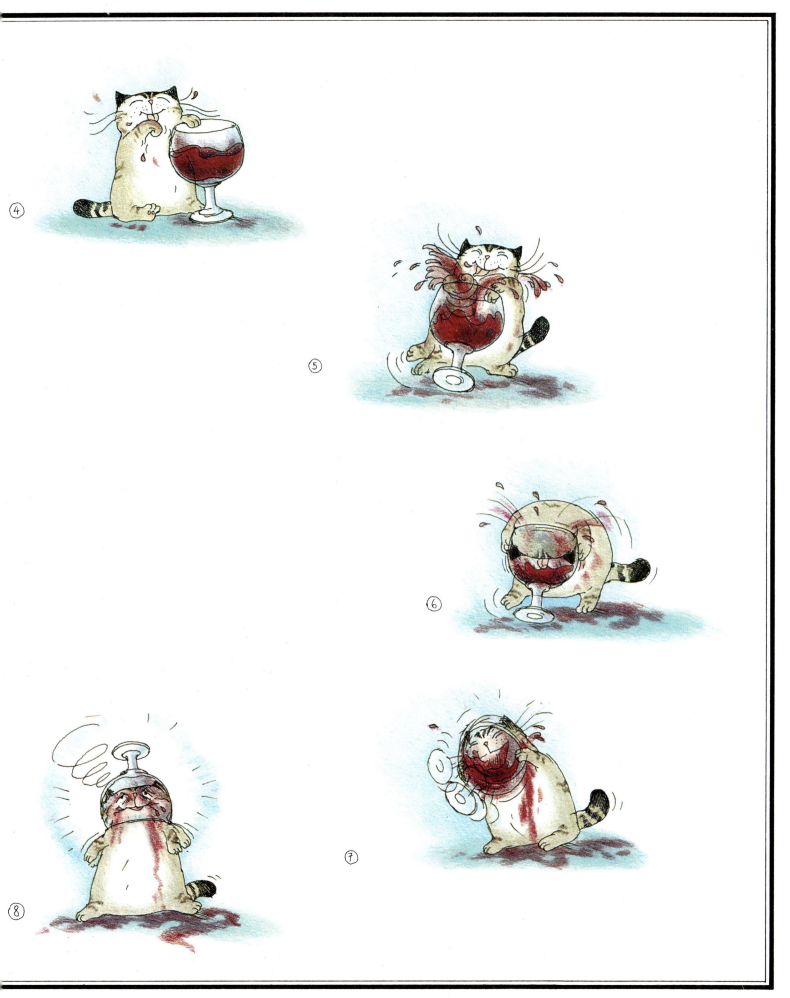

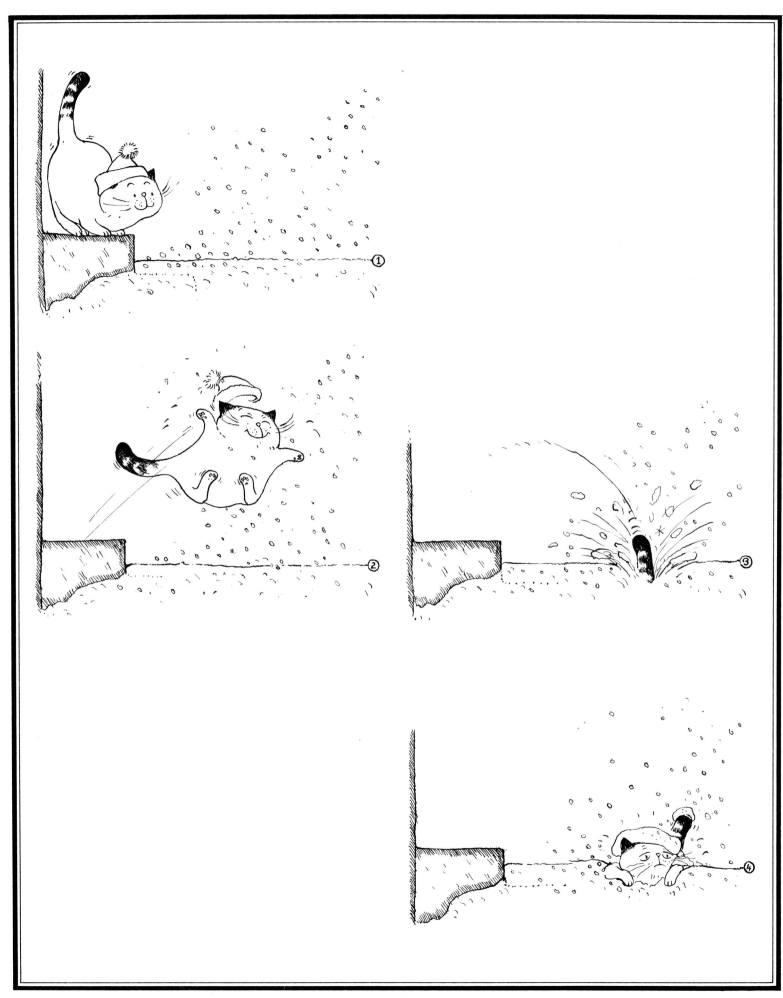

# THE BUNNY RABBIT

My Human laughs a lot. He seems to be happy almost all the time; except, of course, when I do something he doesn't like. Most of the time, I like to hear him laugh. But sometimes he laughs at the wrong thing.

For example, one day some funny white stuff began falling from the sky. It fell and fell until it covered the ground. My Human took me and put me right in the stuff, and it was all cold and wet and nasty. I wanted to get back into the house in the worst way, but I couldn't get out of the stuff. Every time I tried to jump out of it, I'd sink right back. So, I had to jump higher and higher until I finally made it back to the door.

Well, my Human laughed so hard that he fell down right into the white stuff. And he kept yelling, "He's jumping just like a bunny rabbit! A bunny rabbit!" Now, I don't know what a bunny rabbit is, but I'm sure it's an insult to be called one.

Naturally, I had to punish my Human for this. I didn't talk to him for a whole day, and he got very depressed about it. But every once in a while I heard him make a soft, funny noise, like he was laughing to himself.

SVEN

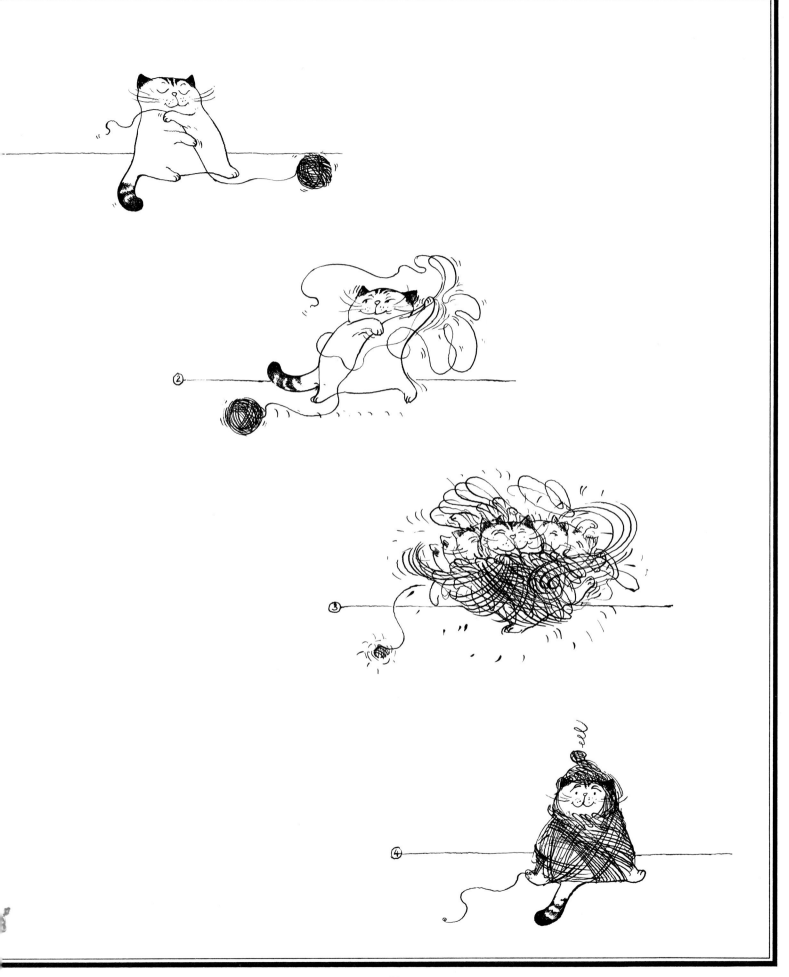

# THE BLACK THING

THERE are a lot of strange things about my Human. For one thing, he's very moody. Sometimes I'll do something that makes him laugh. Then, when I do the same thing a few hours later, he starts screaming and yelling. That's what I call a real defect in his character.

LET me give you an example. There is a black, fuzzy thing that my Human keeps on the floor next to his bed. He puts his feet on it when he gets up in the morning. I fight a lot with this thing. First, I go out into the hallway so that I can get a running start for the attack. Then I crouch down and make myself real small so the thing won't see me. Finally, I launch the attack, darting down the hall and through the bedroom door until, in one fantastic leap, I land on top of the thing. It struggles and tries to get away, but I hold on with all my might. We fight around the room and crash against the furniture and walls, and I'm often completely underneath the thing. But I never give up. Sooner or later, the thing stops moving, and I know I've won again.
My Human always laughs and makes a big to-do over my victory. After all, the black thing is much bigger than I am.

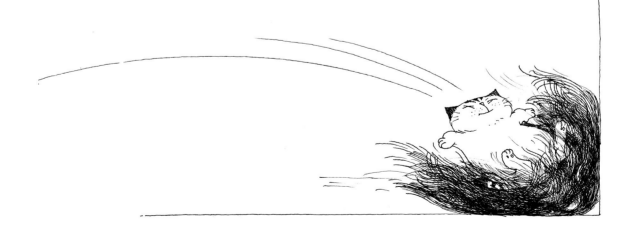

**W**ELL, last night I had a terrible fight with it. Just when I was on the point of winning, my Human made some really horrible sounds, dragged me off the thing, and threw me out of the bedroom. Then he slammed the door shut behind me. You should have seen his face. It was really — well, inhuman. That just goes to show you how moody he can be.

I wonder if he likes that black thing better than me?

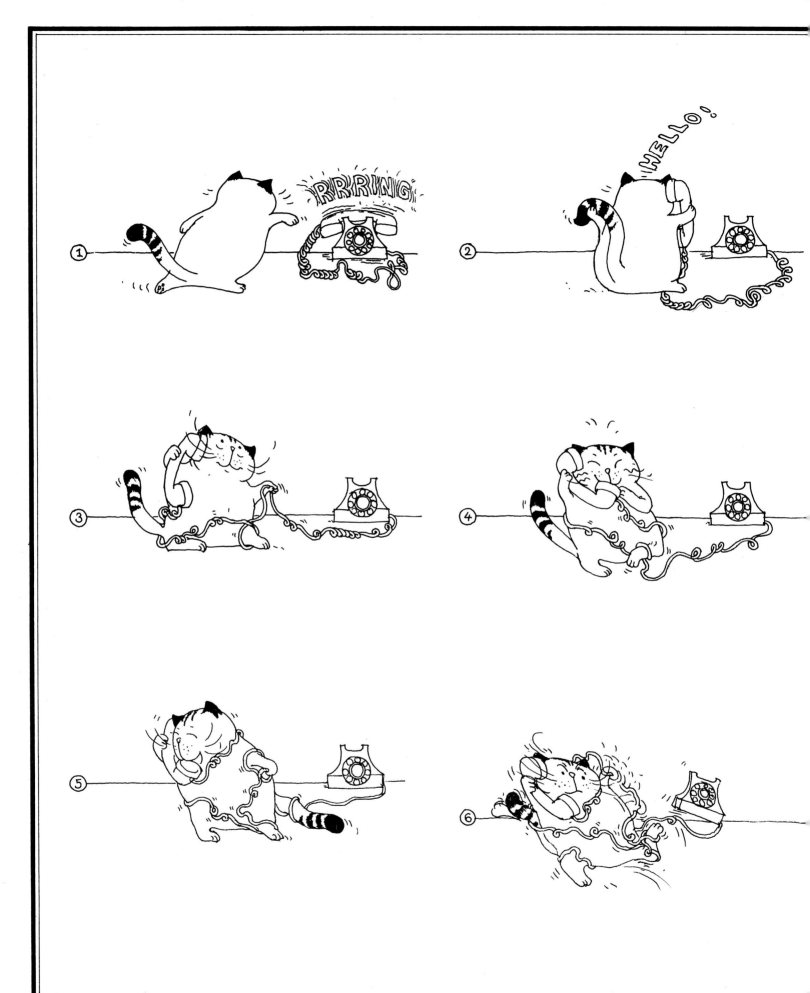

# PINK RIBBONS AND THINGS

I don't know why my Human has so much trouble understanding my games. Maybe he just isn't all that bright.

There's a little room in our house that has a funny white chair in it. My Human sits in the chair every morning. Sometimes he reads, and sometimes he pets me. Sooner or later, he does something that makes the chair sing in a watery voice. This makes me pretty nervous because I don't know what's going on. I think the chair is probably complaining because my Human doesn't want to sit there any longer.

Anyhow, I went into the little room one day when my Human wasn't home. There was a big roll of pink paper ribbon hanging from the wall. I put my claws out just a little and touched the ribbon. A piece of it came off and fell on the floor. I kept touching it and more pieces kept falling. They were pretty, and I wanted to do something with them to please my Human; so I carefully arranged the pieces all over the house, on furniture and on the floor, where he'd be sure to see them right away.

But I guess I did something wrong, because when he came home, he wasn't pleased at all. Maybe I didn't arrange the pieces of pink ribbon in the right way. At any rate, he looked really mad and kept saying bad things in a low voice while he picked up the pieces.

Today I tried to do better. My Human has a bunch of tall, skinny things that he keeps in a vase. They look like flowers; but they're all dry and don't have any smell, so I guess they're not flowers. He's had these things a long time, and he always keeps them in the same vase — which just shows how much imagination humans have.

So I took these things — boy, did they rustle! — and very carefully arranged them all over the house, one here, one there, and so forth. When my Human comes home, he'll be able to see them wherever he looks, and he'll be able to enjoy them that much more. Also, I can play with them better that way. I wonder why he never thought of that?

I'm sure he'll be glad I did it.
Maybe he won't even care that I broke the vase a little while I was working. It must have been a hundred years old anyway.

# THE FAT YELLOW DOT

It's really hard to figure Humans out. Take the case of the black dots and the fat yellow dot.
The black dots fly around in the air and then land on almost everything.
It's fun to catch them, and they buzz and crunch when I bite them.

My Human usually likes it when I catch these black dots. But sometimes he yells at me
for catching them. In the kitchen, the dots fly around and land on the window curtain. Then I
have to make holes — very small holes, really — in the curtain to grab them. Then the yelling
starts. I don't understand why. The holes make it easier to catch the dots; and
besides, you can see outside so much better.

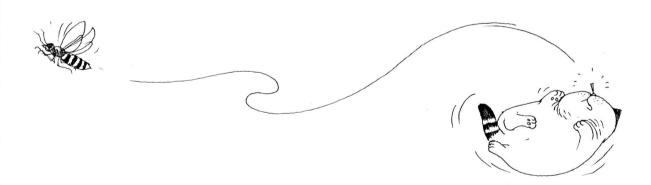

Once a fat yellow dot flew into the house. It was much bigger than the black dots, and
it buzzed a lot louder too. I thought my Human would like me to catch it,
so I tried; but the yellow dot bit me on the nose.
Let me tell you, it really hurt. I ran around the house rubbing my nose,
thinking that I'd get some sympathy. But all my Human did was
laugh, and laugh, and laugh.

A little while later, when he had gone out for a while, I jumped up on top of this table where my Human draws lines on paper with a little stick and then colors the paper. First, I pushed all the papers off the table; then I dropped the little sticks on top of them. There were really a lot of them. I made neat piles on the floor with some of them, but I hid some of the sticks in different places in the room. There was also a square rubber thing that my Human rubs on the paper. I played with it for a while and finally decided to keep it for myself. It'll make a nice toy for when my Human is not home.

When my Human got back, there was a lot of screaming and stomping around. It looked like he was playing hide-and-seek all by himself. I just sat in the kitchen quietly, drinking my milk and pretending not to know anything about it. After all, he can't prove it was me.

This is a very important step in training Humans properly. If they misbehave, they should be punished. Next time a fat yellow dot bites me, I'll bet my Human doesn't even smile.

# MORE ABOUT TRAINING

It's hard work training my Human, but it's worth it.
He is very grateful and gives me good things to eat every single day.
That shows how well he's trained.

It doesn't come to him naturally, though. Maybe it's because he doesn't
drink milk, or even water. At least I've never seen him. What
he drinks is some hot black stuff that smells horrible. And sometimes he
drinks something else out of a bottle that you can see through. That smells bad too.
It looks like water, only more yellow. He tried to give me a taste once, but I wouldn't take it.
Just the smell is enough to make my fur stand on end.

Sometimes I think my Human drinks too much of this yellow stuff. He
sings loud songs and doesn't act like himself. When he's like that, I won't even let him
come close to me, let alone pet me.

either walk away in disgust, or sit on top of the dresser and stare at him until he's ashamed. You have to draw the line somewhere.

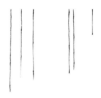

THE next day he's all right again, so he must know that I don't like him when he drinks too much of the yellow water. He looks at me as though he's begging me to forgive him. Of course, I always do. You have to know when to be strict and when to be forgiving.

T'S all part of the training. I know that he always behaves himself for a long time after that.

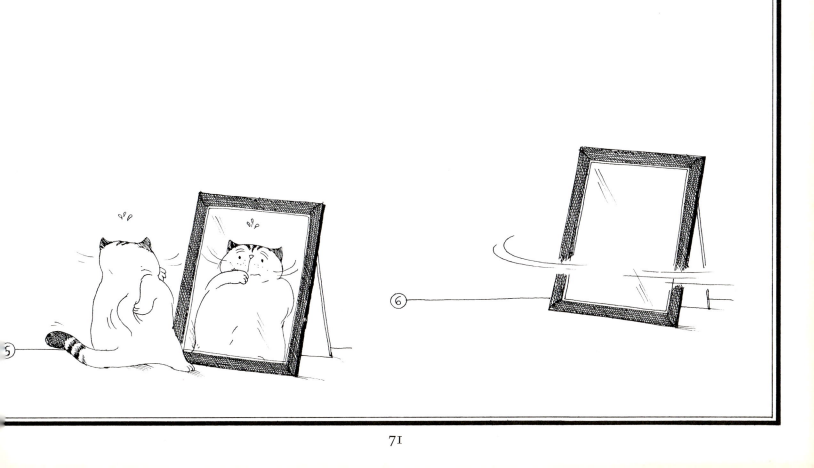

# I MAKE A TERRIBLE DISCOVERY

A terrible thing happened yesterday.
I'm still confused about it, and I don't know where to begin.

First of all, my Human is always playing with these little sticks. He sits at his table
and puts lines on the paper with them, and sometimes he colors
around the lines. He has a funny smile on his face when he
plays with the sticks.

I often wondered why he smiled like that, and yesterday I decided to find out. As soon as I
was alone in the house, I jumped up on the table and took a close look at the
papers. The lines looked something like an animal with four paws,
two pointed ears, and a tail. But what an ugly animal it was!
Just then my Human came home. I was scared because he doesn't like me to sit on his
table. But it was too late to jump off, and so I sat still as though I belonged there.

My Human came closer. At first, I thought he was going to push me off the table.
Instead, he smiled and pointed to the ugly animal made of lines.
"Jacob," he said, "that's you."

I jumped off the table and ran to hide in the bedroom. I was really mad, and the fact that my Human didn't even try to coax me out from under the bed made me even madder. I didn't even come out for dinner. After a while, I heard my Human going out again.

I crept back to the table. The horrible animal lines were still there.
Could that really be me?
WHAT an insult!
I ran over to the mirror. No, I told myself, that's not me. I don't look at all like that line thing. To make sure, I went back to the table and looked at some more of the papers. They all had line animals on them, but the animals were doing dumb things that I would never do. How could my Human say that it was me?

At first, I decided never to speak to him again, but when I thought about it some more I made up my mind to forgive him. My Human is good to me, and I don't want to be too hard on him. Those are just silly lines on paper; and ugly, too.
I guess he isn't able to do any better.

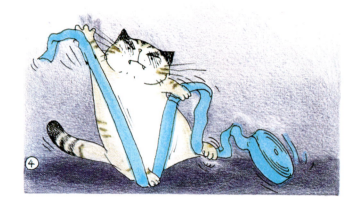

# THE END OF THE DAY

WHEN all is said and done, I have to admit that I really am fond of my Human. He's a good Human and obeys most of the time. Of course, I give him a lot of freedom. I even let him yell at me sometimes and chase me. Otherwise, he'd become too dependent on me. Besides, he needs the exercise, and yelling strengthens his lungs. But it's hard work taking care of a Human, and at night I'm usually dead tired.

THEN I sit in his lap, and he takes his soft paw and scratches me behind the ears and between the eyes. With his other paw, he keeps making lines on his paper . . .

HE must be happy then, because he has a funny smile.
AND I'm happy too, but of course I mustn't tell him so.

First U.S. Edition 1980 by
Barron's Educational Series, Inc.
113 Crossways Park Drive
Woodbury, New York 11797

© 1974, 1977 BENTELI VERLAG,
3011 Berne, Switzerland.
The title of the German edition is:
Jakob—Kleine Katzengeschichten

All rights reserved. No part of this book
may be reproduced or utilized in any form
or by any means, electronic or mechanical,
including photocopying, recording or by
any other information, storage and retrieval
system, without permission in writing
from the Publisher.

International Standard Book No. 0-8120-2290-4

PRINTED IN HONG KONG